Boy and the Seed

By Adam Khedoori

Dedications and Gratitude
Thank you readers!

Thank you for investing in the future.
Thanks to my wife and role models, who help me make life wonderful.
Thanks to my children who give me inspiration to improve myself. Thank you to my wonderful family who has given me so much. Thanks to all who helped make this book possible. Thanks to the great teachers of this world who are here to guide us! Thanks Creator for giving us life!

Copyright © 2020 Adam Khedoori

Book: ISBN - 978-0-6488457-6-8

First published 2020 by Think and Grow Publishing © Sydney, Australia

Authored by **Adam Khedoori (Australia)**
Edited by **Renee Kurz (Australia), Zahara Francisco (Philippines), Kathy Beckman (USA), Adam Khedoori (Australia), Anita Khedoori**

Illustrations by **Prabir Sarkar (India)**
Layout by **Kashif Tahir (Pakistan)**

Inspiration quotes the seeds of success

"A good quote can sink into the heart and plant a seed and bring out our best qualities. Think about one a day and make your mind shine!" **Adam Khedoori**

"If you are willing to do only what's easy, life will be hard. But if you're willing to do what's hard, life will be easy." **T. Harv Eker**

"Whether you think you can, or you think you can't- You're right." **Henry Ford**

"Formal education will make you a living, self-education will make you a fortune."
"If you really want to do something, you'll find a way. If you don't, you'll find an excuse." **Jim Rohn**

"We cannot always build a future for our youth, but we can always build our youth for the future." **Franklin D. Roosevelt**

"When educating the minds of our youth, we must not forget to educate their hearts." **Dalai Lama**

"The youth is the hope of our future." **Jose Rizal**

"Whatever the mind can conceive and believe, the mind can achieve."
Napoleon Hill

"When we are no longer able to change a situation, we are challenged to change ourselves."
"Everything can be taken from a person but one thing: the last of the human freedoms-to choose one's attitude in any given set of circumstances, to choose one's own way."
"Between stimulus and response there is a space. In that space is our power to choose our response. In our response lies our growth and our freedom."
Viktor Frankl

Once upon a time, a boy was playing in a big grass field. He ran around trying to catch butterflies. But, he could never quite catch one, as they always flew away.

The boy saw a beautiful flower in the field. He stopped and stared and wondered what made this flower grow.

So, He asked his mother,
"What makes a flower grow?
"A flower starts from a
seed," his mother said.
"What is a seed?" the boy
replied.

"A seed can grow into a flower, do you want to try to grow a flower?" The boy's eyes lit up and he became really excited. So they went to a store to get the things they needed.

They got some seeds,
soil, a small pot and a
watering spray bottle.

On the way home, the boy asked, "How does a seed turn into a flower?" The mother said with a warm voice, "A seed first needs love, it needs to be nurtured in the right place, given the right amount of water, and it must also grow in its season." The boy was a bit confused. *A seed needs all those things to grow, he thought.*

They got home and the boy was eager to start. The mother looked at the boy with gentle eyes and said, "It's not the right time to grow a flower yet, we will have to wait for 2 weeks until spring." The boy puzzled, looked down, and said in a sad tone "Ok, I can wait."

Two weeks went, "Mom, it's time, spring is here!" The mother said, "OK." The mother showed the boy what to do. They got 3 pots and filled them with soil.

Then, she opened the seed packet and poured the tiny seeds into her hand. "How will a seed grow into a flower?" he asked curiously. To which his mother repeated, "A seed needs love, nurturing in the right place and the right amount of water. And flowers will need to grow at their own pace, growth will always go in stages, and then it will become a beautiful flower"

The mom told the boy to poke a little hole on the soil with his finger, place the seed inside and put some water on it. Then the boy said, "I want one in my room." With loving eyes, the mother replied, "Great! Let's put one outside and the other on the kitchen window."

The boy and his mother placed the pots around the house. "Water them everyday with just a few sprays." The mother told the boy.

After 2 weeks, something happened!
One of the seeds changed shape and
opened. However, nothing happened to
the other two. "How does a seed grow?"
said the curious boy. "The other two are
still stuck."The mother replied, "A seed
needs love, nurturing in the right place
with the right amount of water."

The boy wondered why the one in the kitchen grew. He saw that the sun was shining on the pot. And went to his bedroom, got the pot and placed it by the window. Two days later, the seed opened and started to sprout!

But the boy's third seed was still not coming out. Once again, he asked his mother who repeated, "A seed first needs love, it needs nurturing in the right place, and the right amount of water."

The boy asked, "How can I give the seed love?" The mother said, looking at the sad boy, "This pot outside needs extra love because it's very hot and it needs to get more water every day to grow."

Smiling, the boy rushed to spray the pot
2 times a day. Then two days later, the
boy saw the seed opening just like the
others. He got excited and watched the
plant grow every day.

He wanted the flowers to grow faster! But he thought about what his mother said, "The flowers will need to grow at their own pace, growth will always go in stages, and then it will become a beautiful flower"

One day, the boy saw a flower blooming from his plant and he knew how a flower grew. "A seed first needs love, nurturing in the right place and the right amount of water, then it grows in stages."

Then, as he was looking at the flower, a butterfly came and landed on it.

The boy was very happy and left the butterfly to enjoy resting on his flower.

The end.

About the Author

'Adam Khedoori'

Adam spent many years on a quest to find great teachers in this world and share their work.

He's an author, a publisher, and co-partner to LeRoy Malouf to present the Positive Power of Being Neutral (PPBN) Udemy© www.udemy.com

He works as a healer at: www.clearlifenow.com

Adam's goal is to share his findings through picture books for the youth, parents and educators to learn how they can all develop a mind of self-growth and succeed in life, through the study of great people. Adam lives happily in Sydney, Australia with his wife, Anita and their 3 boys.

Follow **Think and Grow Publishing** on
Facebook: @DreamBelieveCreate2020
www.thinkgrowpublish.com

Introduction to Thought Leader Series

Dear readers,

Welcome to **Think and Grow Publishing's** first set of books.

These books are a little different so I would like to point out how you can get the most from reading them. My books are intended to provide parents, care-givers, educators and children, mental and emotional nutrition for fostering growth, happiness, and success in life.

The motto is:
Dream it, Believe it and Create it

Each book is planting seeds that will be able to sprout given the right efforts and a **Think and Grow formula.**

• **Dream:** Think deeply about what you want to achieve. Be positive and do not state things in a negative way, don't see things worse than they are. Instead, try to see things clearly and without judgment. Dream how you want it to be. 'See things being on the way, not in the way', by Dr.John Demartini

• **Believe:** Feel joy in your heart. When you have a goal to improve yourself or make life better for others, then your dream becomes aligned with 'making life wonderful' as Dr Marshall Rosenberg says is the purpose of life. You will have the energy to learn and develop yourself, 'You can be the person you can become' says Ryuho Okawa.

• **Create:** Take action to realize your dream. It requires patience, love, self-reflection, continual learning, change, and determination. Yes, life can be wonderful when you take just a little time each day to fill it up with the joy of self-improvement. Remember to just take one step at a time, and even if set-backs occur, keep searching and going forward.

About the style of this book and how you can get the best use out of it...

Firstly, there is an illustrated story with a message and ways to be happy, I have spent many years finding the root causes of problems in life and found a few hints for success and progress. Just like Bill Phillips said, "Focus on progress, not perfection."

Secondly, I introduce you to a thought leader who has found a way to make life wonderful in an area of life.

Thirdly, I will write a life changing essay in each book.

And finally, I share comments about the work of the thought leader and some basic principles.

Most importantly, I wish you to enjoy the experience and naturally sprout seeds in the garden of you and your children's minds. I hope that these books become the fertilizer to start a life of self-development, gratitude, and joyful living. You can create a magnificent garden in your mind!

With all my love.

Adam David Khedoori

Think and grow publishing values

Our values create our stories and drive us towards our goals. Values determine our actions and what we are doing right now.

Effort
Make no effort is to make no progress.

Desire
Hunger towards achieving success.

Progress
Knowing the final goals, not about perfection it's about progress.

Resilience
The noun resilience stems from the Latin resilience "to rebound, recoil." Resilience is a person's mental ability to recover quickly from misfortune, illness or depression and bounce back.

Courage
The axe in your tool belt to cut down the physical, mental and emotional walls blocking the path, that leads to growth and progress.

Happiness
The goal of life, knowing values and actions to make life wonderful, having a mind of giving, understanding the laws of cause and effect on mind.

Adversity
Trials and tests that are here to support us and make us stronger.

Strength
A capacity to know our limits and push through them, linked with progress, resilience, and courage.

Love
Love means to give without expecting anything in return, When we do things from a loving place and not to "get", we find that love flows.

Forgiveness
Forgiving ourselves or others from mistakes and learning from them.

Growth
An inevitable part of life, we can stagnate, get complacent or we can choose growth and find joy in learning and developing ourselves.

Self reflection
A chance to undo the past, make peace, and re-align with our goals of progress. We can change how we feel about an event or a person by thinking of the meaning behind it. It's not always about what happened, it's about how we feel about it.

Self-help spirit
The spirit to take responsibility for our life, learning and opportunities. The feeling of pride in our own efforts.

Responsibility
Acting in response to a cause and the ability to return to love, support, strength and progress.

Gratitude
Gratitude means to be thankful for all that we have been given. Even for small things we can feel grateful for. Take 5 mins a day to think about things that help you.

Self-discipline
One of the most important skills we need to master in order to accomplish anything in life. The ability to do what you need to do, when it needs to be done, whether you like it or not. This is biggest key to opening a door to our success.

If you are willing to do only what's easy, life will be hard. But if you are willing to do what's hard, life will be easy.

T. Harv Eker

Life Changing Essay
Stages of Love, Nurture and Forgive

Please note The boy and the seed could also be changed to The girl and the seed.

What makes this story special?
Is it the boy's curiosity?
Is it the warm and gentle guidance from the mother?
Is it the process of allowing nature to change shape?

I have been studying and using the methods described in this book, and noticed the difference in my life. I learned these teachings from Master Ryuho Okawa. He contemplated the phrase below for a few years.

Love people, Nurture people, Forgive people.
Master Ryuho Okawa

He describes in his book, **Love, Nurture, and Forgive** that to love means to give without expecting anything in return. For him, this is the primary cause of most of life's sufferings, which I also discovered in positive thinking psychology. Even positive thinking can cause us to suffer. But why!?

You wished to get a good mark on a test and you wanted a person to like you, you needed your friend or family to help you with something and each time you didn't get the results you thought you would get. Then disappointment or other negative emotions come up inside of us. Yes, positive thinking can sometimes lead to disappointment. As I explain in detail in my course with LeRoy Malouf about the Positive Power of Being Neutral (PPBN) on Udemy.com when we only think positively about things. We can end up in a see-saw when we think we are high in the air, but no one is on the other side and we fall to the ground. I am saying we should be able to look and accept the other side, the negative side. We don't focus on the negative side so long that we get stuck with negative thinking either, we just have to be able to look at two sides of a situation. Which is the key to be able to look at both sides and then reach a **balanced state of mind.**

Disappointments are temporary setbacks are going to be part of the process. If you read the values in this book, you will find the value for Adversity which states that trials and tests that are here to support us and make us stronger. **Adversity** is a setback and we feel it deep inside. We may feel like giving up, we may want to change, or we may even just be happy to stop at our current level. However, it's here for our growth and development.

Love simply means to give, and love dies when we expect things back from others. The next stage of love is nurturing as you see in the story, the mother had knowledge of growing a plant from a seed and instructed the boy on the care and support needed for a seed to grow.

The knowledge used in the story was converted to wisdom by applying and going through some setbacks and working out the issues. I once heard the golden rule was to do to others as you would have them do to you. However, we all have different tastes and things we like. So we can do our best to know what the other person really wants. And think in terms of **Doing unto others as they want done to them** is the new golden rule.

An important part of nurturing is also setting healthy boundaries or limits. Science says that limits give a good framework for children to flourish. For parents here is the link for understanding more about limits.
https://www.handinhandparenting.org/2017/03/types-of-limits-kids-need/

Many people talk of unconditional love, which is the next stage of love known as forgiveness. Forgiveness simply means to let go of right and wrong, realise that we all make mistakes, work on understanding each other more deeply, remember that each of us is originally good and has a good heart. Each of us can learn from any event in life. Each of us will encounter many setbacks.

Master Ryuho Okawa states, "Start from practicing the 'love that gives,' instead of expecting something in return, you can experience a remarkable transformation through your self-help efforts to develop through the stages of love."

Remember that it's a continual cycle that we continually go through, as we pass through loving, nurturing, and forgiving, which brings the ultimate happiness that is felt deep in the heart when we realise the way to progress through the stages of love.

Adam Khedoori

Forgiveness can take time, and it's part of accepting things as they are and realizing that mistakes are part of the process.
Adam Khedoori

Thought leader – Napoleon Hill

One of the greatest thinkers and teachers of success

> We are the Masters of our fate, the Captains of our Souls because we have the power to control our thoughts.
> **Napoleon Hill**

In 1937, a book was born and continued to be sold in bookshops today. That book is the **'Think and Grow Rich' by Napoleon Hill**. Millions of readers have used the principles in the book to make their life wonderful!

Hill was put on a quest by one of the richest men of his time, Andrew Carnegie without being paid a cent. Why didn't he pay him? And what was the quest?

The quest to find out the keys to success and what are the principles. He had just a short time to decide, then with Andrew Carnegie's help, he was able to interview the top 500 most successful people in the world at the turn of the 1900s and find out just what success is. He did find the causes for success and wrote about them. Hill wasn't paid for taking the challenge from Andrew Carniege, which gave him even more determination to complete this work and its principles. His books helped many people rise from all fall in life. Aside from **Think and Grow Rich**, He also wrote the **Laws of Success in 16 Lessons, Grow Rich with Peace of Mind**, and the provocative **Outwitting the Devil**.

Hill put his life work into the Science of Success, the Philosophy of Achievement, and found the laws that govern them. The main message is summarised in his **13 Principles of Think and Grow Rich**.

What are some of the key lessons we can learn from Hill's works?

What can we learn from successful people? Hill states, "A burning desire to be, and to do is the starting point from which all dreamers must take off. Dreams are not born of indifference, laziness, or lack of ambition". Hill also taught about resilience and bounce-back ability.

> When defeat comes, accept it as a signal that your plans are not sound, rebuild those plans, and set sail once again toward your coveted goal.
> **Napoleon Hill**

When creating a mindset that is capable of accomplishing anything, keeping it clear of negativity is paramount. Where negativity dwells, fear causes doubt, which will eventually murder all grand ideas, chances of prosperity or happiness.

---

https://www.thebusinessquotes.com/napoleon-hill-quotes/

An effective tool to keep fear at bay is to bathe in positive thoughts as often as possible. "It is essential for you to encourage positive emotions as dominant forces of your mind, and discourage – and eliminate negative emotions," Hill states. What is the purpose of setbacks and adversity? "**Every adversity, every failure, every heartache** carries with it the seed of an equal or **greater benefit**."

One driving force inside us is imagination, which comes from thoughts. Walt Disney knew about the power of imagination, creating a cartoon into a land and world theme park and building one of the biggest brands in the world, saying, "If you can dream it, you can do it." Albert Einstein also taught about the superpowers of creation. "**Imagination** is more important than knowledge. For knowledge is limited, whereas **imagination** embraces the entire world, stimulating progress, giving birth to evolution." Also, saying in short, "Imagination is everything." One of my favorite beliefs of Hill's work is "Whatever the mind of man can conceive and believe, it can achieve." I have proven this true in my life many times. By having desires, thinking, and acting on them and having them realised in real life.

Hill teaches the road to success in the **Think and Grow Rich** book, and it's one of the most important books to read for all students in life. On the road to success, we will want to make progress, but remember there are two ways to progress in life, one is by making mistakes by trial and error or from people who have made them. It's far less painful to learn from others' mistakes and it also saves us a lot of time.

There is a powerful recording free on Youtube called **Think and Grow Rich: Instant Motivator**, which is a summary of the book by Earl Nightingale.

It may surprise you but Bruce Lee and Jim Carrey both read and used Hill's formula and it paid off!

The Business Insider also shares the basics of the 13 principles which I believe will apply for many centuries. It's up to anyone who wants to learn and progress in business to see the core of these teachings.

The book has been made into a movie, **Think and Grow Rich: The Legacy by James Whittaker.** Whittaker has interviewed numerous beneficiaries of author Napoleon Hill's insights and explores the impact it has made on their lives. Not all measure their success in purely financial terms, but all credit a belief in themselves and the right mentality to achieve their goals.

I believe Hill's work should be in every business class and reviewed by students in high schools.

If you continue trying even after failing three times, you have the capacity to be a leader. If you keep fighting after failing ten times, you have the nature of a genius
Napoleon Hill

What do you want in life? And What are you prepared to do to get it? .... Are Hill's key points to remember.

Finally, the Hill foundation can be found at www.naphill.org

———————————————

https://www.businessinsider.com.au/napoleon-hill-think-and-grow-rich-2015-7?r=US&IR=T
https://www.smh.com.au/money/planning-and-budgeting/think-and-grow-rich-revisited-20180802-p4zv7t.html

Think and Grow Rich
Short Summary by Paul Minors

https://paulminors.com/blog/think-grow-rich-by-napoleon-hill-book-summary-pdf/

Think And Grow Rich is a state of mind. It exploits the power of thought to manifest strong desires and a definite purpose into reality. Turning your all-consuming obsession (definite purpose) into a reality is not an easy task. However, if the desire is strong and you're willing to raise the stakes, you will win. The author projects the following formula:

Desire + Ideas + Plans + Massive Action = Success

Start with your goal. What do you really want? A better job? To succeed in your current career? To work for a business leader who inspires you?

To achieve that goal, shifting your thinking from failure consciousness to success consciousness is the key. For this to happen, the question 'how do I get a job?' needs to change into 'what can I give to a job?', and 'how do I get more dollars per hour?' into 'how do I give more energy, desire, focus?'

To get from where you are to where you want to be, the author highlights:

> Never quit. Never give up. Focus. Seek help. Make new connections. Take different approaches. Seek additional resources to help you improve your job search skills. Persist and find people who can help you to achieve your goals.

1. DESIRE: The Turning Point Of Achievement

What do you desire above everything else? A powerful desire towards achieving a goal uses a combination of two types of motivation:

Pull motivations	Push motivations
The outcome of the goal is so favourable, that it pulls you towards the goal	You are pushed to action because of the negative consequences of not taking action

The author provides the mindset for **5 key areas of Desire:**

Career

Going from 'what do I get?' to 'how will I grow?' requires shifting from ego-driven concerns (title, salary, benefits etc.) to growth opportunities within the company and position.

Leading
To lead, first, you need to follow and learn from an existing leader. How would it affect your career if you became an apprentice to someone at the top of your field that you admire?

Money
This is a series of steps that the author suggests for money-based desires.

- Be definite as to the amount of money or type of job.
- Determine exactly what you intend to give in return for the money you desire.
- Establish a definite date when you intend to attain the money you desire.
- Create a definite plan for carrying out your desire and begin at once.
- Write out a clear, concise statement of the amount of money you intend to acquire, name the time limit, state what you intend to give in return, and describe the plan through which you plan to accumulate it.
- Read your written statement aloud, twice daily.

Failure
Look for lessons within failure and examine them without the emotional attachment of why something has failed. Use failure as a growth opportunity towards greater accomplishments.

> Every failure brings with it the seed of an equivalent success.

2. FAITH: Visualisation & Belief In Attainment Of Desire

> Your own success or failure is based largely on your self-belief, and a mind-set of positive expectancy is the foundation of which your success can be achieved.

Faith is the starting point of success and the glue that holds it all together. As a state of mind, faith can be induced or created through affirmations or repeated instructions to the subconscious mind. By encouraging positive emotions and eliminating negative emotions (such as doubt, denial, and fear), faith can be a useful tool in various ways:

- It is an antidote for failure.
- By believing in yourself, others will believe in you, too.
- Employers seek successful, confident people who can make a positive impact.

To summon faith in the form of self-confidence, the author suggests that you sign your name to a statement, which you should be repeating daily towards subconsciously influencing your thoughts and actions. This statement should include affirmations that acknowledge certain things about yourself:

- That you have the ability to achieve your purpose.
- That you promise to take action.
- That you understand that your thoughts will gradually transform into a physical reality.
- That you promise to dedicate time to ensuring that these thoughts become real.
- That you understand the importance of self-confidence and promise to spend 10 minutes a day working on this.
- That you will never stop trying to achieve your goals.
- That you are willing to serve others, and in turn will get others to serve you.
- Find examples of people who are where you want to be (career, money, influence-wise, you name it), use their examples as a way to keep your faith strong, and remind yourself that your desire is possible to attain.

3. AUTO-SUGGESTION: The Medium For Influencing The Subconscious

The principle of auto-suggestion communicates our desires directly to the subconscious mind in a spirit of unshakable faith.

Through routine repetition of our conscious thoughts and desires (as mentioned in the ritual of the "Faith" section above) to ourselves, we can regain absolute control over the material which reaches our subconscious mind, exercising control over our decisions, feelings, and actions.

4. SPECIALISED KNOWLEDGE: Personal Experience Or Observations

For our desires to translate into monetary, career, or another kind of success (which we've picked in the "Desire" step), we are first required to have specialised knowledge of the service, product, or profession of which we intend to offer in return for fortune.

Notably, this specialised knowledge doesn't have to be in your possession already. Knowing how to purchase or rent knowledge is a popular way of fulfilling this step. Courses, seminars, books (or summaries!), industry conferences, they all improve your odds of acquiring the much-needed specialised knowledge for yourself.

Working with knowledgeable people ("renting knowledge") is the other equally powerful – side of the spectrum. Lifelong learning is obviously necessary for an ambitious person to keep up with all the latest developments in their field.

5. IMAGINATION: The Workshop Of The Mind

Ideas are products of and given a shape or form through imagination.

The author mentions two types of imagination.

Synthetic imagination: This faculty includes arranging old concepts, ideas or plans into new combinations.

And creative imagination: this faculty is where ideas come from ("infinite intelligence") and "hunches" and "inspirations are received.

To make the best use of your imagination towards achieving your big goal, come up with a list of ideas that will both inspire you and allow you to best utilise your talents.

6. ORGANISED PLANNING: The Crystallisation Of Desire Into Action

Simply hoping to succeed at your goal is not the answer. Every achievement starts with a strong desire, workshopped to reality through imagination, followed by an organised plan.

No plan is perfect. When you execute your plan, you will likely experience a temporary defeat. The best way to approach defeat is to simply accept it as a signal that your plans are not sound. Rebuild your plans and keep pursuing your goal, armed with the knowledge of your previous failures.

Don't give up before you reach your goal, because quitters do not get to see their long-term plans come to fruition.

7. DECISION: The Mastery Of Procrastination

People who fail to succeed, without exception, reach decisions, if at all, very slowly, and change their minds quickly and often. Successful people reach decisions promptly and definitely, changing their mind slowly. They know what they want and, generally, get it. Definiteness of decision always requires courage. Procrastination, the opposite of decision, is a common enemy which practically every person must conquer.

8. PERSISTENCE: The Sustained Effort Necessary To Induce Faith

Lack of persistence is one of the major causes of failure. It can be conquered but this depends entirely upon the intensity of one's desire – weak desires bring weak results. The basis of persistence is the power of will, and it's also influenced by other factors, such as:

• Definiteness of purpose	• Definiteness of plans	• Co-operation
• Self-reliance	• Accurate knowledge	• Habits

Which of the **aforementioned factors are you lacking**, which might be hindering your persistence? On the contrary, lack of persistence begets the following symptoms:

- Wishing instead of willing
- Searching for shortcuts
- Fear of criticism
- Weakness of desire
- Willingness to quit
- Lack of organised plans
- Procrastination
- Lack of interest
- Indecision
- Self-satisfaction
- Indifference

So, how does one develop persistence? The author suggests the **following 4 steps:**

1. Develop a definite purpose, backed by a burning desire for its fulfillment.
2. Build a definite plan, expressed in continuous action.
3. Keep out all negative and discouraging influences.
4. Stay accountable to people who will encourage you to follow through your plan and purpose.

9. POWER OF THE MASTERMIND: The Driving Force

A mastermind is having a team of people in place, whose job it is to help you succeed and carry out your plans. Who could be in your team and how could you form one in the next 30 days? Nobody can acquire great power and succeed without the power of a mastermind. According to the author:

No two minds ever come together without, thereby, creating a third, invisible, intangible force which may be likened to a third mind.

The goal of a mastermind is to convert knowledge into power, by organising it into definite plans, and then translating plans into action.

10. SUBCONSCIOUS MIND: The Connecting Link

The subconscious mind is the connecting link between the finite mind of a human and infinite intelligence.

The subconscious mind can be used as a medium for transmuting your desires into their physical or monetary equivalent. However, if you fail to plant your own desires into it, as a result of your neglect, it will feed upon any thoughts that reach it.

To gain control over your subconscious mind, form the habit of applying and using to your advantage the following 7 major positive emotions: Desire, Faith, Love, Sex, Enthusiasm, Romance, Hope.

The mere presence of a single negative emotion in your conscious mind might be sufficient to destroy all chances of constructive aid from your subconscious mind. The 7 major negative emotions to avoid are; Fear, Jealousy, Hatred, Revenge, Greed, Superstition, Anger.

Eventually, the positive emotions will dominate your mind completely, so that the negative ones cannot enter.

11. THE BRAIN: A Broadcasting And Receiving Station For Thought

Every human brain is both a broadcasting and receiving station for the vibration of thought.

The subconscious mind is the "sending station" of the brain, through which vibrations of thought are broadcast. The creative imagination is the "receiving set," through which the vibrations of thought are picked up from the ether.

When stimulated ("stepped up") to a high rate of vibration, the mind becomes more receptive to the vibration of thought. This "stepping up" takes place through positive or negative emotions.

Vibrations of an exceedingly high rate are the only vibrations picked up and carried, by the ether, from one brain to another.

12. THE SIXTH SENSE: The Door To The Temple Of Wisdom

The understanding of the sixth sense comes only by meditation, through mind development from within.

Once you've mastered the sixth sense, you will be able to receive warnings about impending dangers in time to avoid them and get notified of opportunities in time to embrace them.

However, the sixth sense will never function if indecision, doubt, and fear remain in your mind. They are closely related: indecision crystallises into doubt, and the two blend to become the end result, fear.

The 6 basic fears are; Poverty, Criticism, Ill Health, Loss of love, Old age, Death. However, there's also a 7th 'enemy': susceptibility to negative influences.

To shield yourself from this enemy, like all people who accumulate great riches, you have to:

- Put your willpower into constant use, until you build immunity against negative influences in your own mind,
- Deliberately seek the company of people who influence you to think and act from a positive standpoint, and
- Use your willpower to gain control over your thoughts and influence your subconscious mind.
- Fear is just a state of mind. It is subject to control and direction. Use this knowledge to your advantage.

> Man's thought impulses begin immediately to translate themselves into their physical equivalent, whether those thoughts are voluntary or involuntary.

CONCLUSION: Key takeaways

- The book exploits the power of thought to manifest strong desires and a definite purpose into reality.
- Faith is the glue that holds it all together.
- Every achievement starts with a strong desire, workshopped to reality through imagination, followed by an organised plan.
- Successful people reach decisions promptly and definitely, changing their mind slowly.
- Lack of persistence is one of the major causes of failure.
- To acquire great power & succeed, you need the help of a mastermind.
- Sexual drive, transmuted into creative and productive outlets, can be a powerful force for success.
- Fear is just a state of mind. It is subject to control and direction.

Further reading

How To Win Friends And Influence People by Dale Carnegie. As relevant as ever before, Dale Carnegie's principles endure and will help you achieve your maximum potential in the complex and competitive modern age.

If you are interested in the money side of things, **Rich Dad Poor Dad** is a really interesting perspective on lessons learned from a Rich Man and a Poor Man. This book by Robert T Kiyosaki includes helpful tips on how to translate these lessons into real life and become rich yourself!

Guidelines is my eBook that summarises the main lessons from 33 of the best-selling self-help books in one place. It is the ultimate book summary; Available as an 80-page ebook and 115-minute audiobook. Guidelines lists 31 rules (or guidelines) that you should follow to improve your productivity, become a better leader, do better in business, improve your health, succeed in life and become a happier person.

It's worth-while to keep a copy of this book and review it periodically over a few years.

Action Steps

1. Think about your burning desire you seek to accomplish.
2. Create a definite plan to carry out and set a deadline for it.
3. Form a mastermind of people to hold you accountable.
4. Download the complete book on Amazon.

All Feedback is encouraged with gratitude!

Dear readers,

Thank you so much for taking the time to read and discover the great people featured in this book. I hope this story will assist and plant a seed in your child's mind for infinite growth and success in their future.

I would love to get your feedback, Positive I hope… if you have any ideas or criticism let me know directly via Feedback on www.goodreads.com search "Adam Khedoori" you will see all my books there and on Facebook page:
Facebook[@DreamBelieveCreate2020]

If you think this book is useful and helpful to your school, community, friends or family please share it with them. Our mission is to bring a bright future towards the world and make this world a wonderful place planting positive seeds one at a time.

Sending a big THANK YOU and letting you know I BELIEVE EVERYONE IS GOOD INSIDE!